The
Thousand Island
Heroes

The Thousand Island Heroes

L.S. Bakhai

authorHOUSE®

Dearest Amber,
wishing you all the happiness, love and
laughter through all of your own
life adventures! With love from Lepa

AuthorHouse™ UK
1663 Liberty Drive
Bloomington, IN 47403 USA
www.authorhouse.co.uk
Phone: 0800.197.4150

Published by AuthorHouse 02/22/2016

ISBN: 978-1-5049-8764-6 (sc)
ISBN: 978-1-5049-8763-9 (e)

Print information available on the last page.

This book is printed on acid-free paper.

CHAPTER

1

Deep below the world of humans, lived the Thousand Islanders. Full of vitality and goodness, they were a friendly bunch. Today was a particularly exciting day at Worcester High School. It was the last day before eight full weeks of summer holidays bringing a promise of fun and freedom to all the Thousand Island children.

Arti Choke was brimming with excitement as he thought about his summer plans with his best friends, Kai and Ginger and his adopted sister, Ivy Gourd. Head of the basketball team, dedicated to doing his best in class, big brother to five younger brothers and Ivy, Arti was always full of energy. To celebrate their last day, he had organised a picnic and afternoon of games.

"Let's get going to the park then!" Ginger shouted. She was loud enough for the whole school to hear. Looking at her, she was just as vibrant physically as she was in personality. With piercing eyes, wild, long ginger hair flowing down her back and a luminous smile, she always made her presence known. And with her often wrapping her school tie around the front of her head, talking with her hands on her hips and striding forward like a soldier, she appeared to always be charging ahead.

Arti was right, it was a perfect picnic day. The sun's rays flowed through the trees and forced their way through the park. The blue of the sky was piercing, almost as bright as the sun itself and the fact that there was not one cloud in the sky made the blend of yellow and blue even more intense. It was hot but the air still skipped past the Thousand Islanders, spraying them with a light breeze. The gang splashed each other with water from the fountain, ran around playing silly games without rules and talked about what they were going to do for the rest of summer. They were so relaxed and enjoying themselves, that they didn't notice the sinister figures from the evil Mould Island hovering around them.

An hour later, as the sun began its descent in the distant, the group prepared to leave. As they packed up under the big oak tree, Ivy handed Arti something from her bag.

"Here you go" she said, putting it in Arti's lap.

"What's this?" he asked and as he spoke, unravelled a long purple and black liquorice roll.

"It's Kazai, my liquorice roll pet. I was hiding him from mum and dad because I can't control him. I thought you'd be good at straightening him out."

Arti was just about to protest about the unruliness of Ivy's pet, it seemed perfectly quiet and calm. Just then, the roll (or Kazai as Ivy lovingly called him) started making all sorts of manic movements.

"He likes you!" Ivy gushed. Six years younger than everyone else, Ivy was Arti's biggest fan. She followed him wherever he went and Arti, being the protective brother that he was, loved having her close by him. Ivy was slightly more on the tubby side and much shorter than her brother, with a delicate face. Long eyelashes, a cute button nose and a sweet smile made it difficult for anyone to say no to her. A ray of sunshine for Arti and his friends, she would often amuse them with silly rhymes and jokes, giggling with the most infectious laugh anyone had heard.

Arti, now struggling to control Kazai, forced him back into the bag.

"Seems a bit too energetic for me, I think I already have my hands full with you!"

Suddenly, Arti heard a strange noise coming from behind the tree. Something was rustling nearby. He turned around to investigate.

"Did you hear that weird noise?" he asked Ivy. She didn't reply.

"Ivy, did you hear that?" he repeated. He still didn't get a response and turned to ask her a third time. But it was too late, she was gone.

"Dear Arti.... I am writing with regards to your sister Ivy who you may have noticed is missing. No, no, that won't do. I want it to be a little more poetic, I mean it might be worth a lot of money in the future, a collector's piece. With so many people reading it, I have to give it that lasting impression."

Sitting on a throne in his castle on Mould Island, Mr Mould was dictating a letter to send to Arti. As usual, he was more involved in his own glory than the purpose of the letter. At the tender age of 74,362, it was fair to say there wasn't much attractive about him. Mr Mould was uglier than anything else in existence. With long, flat feet and a greenish brown skin tone making up a thin layer of slippery smooth fur, he was not someone you warmed to. He was as creepy as the lank, greasy vines hanging over his greying castle. He was slimy like the green gunk which bubbled in the moat. His face was as furry as the fluffy growth which festered deep in the gardens. He hated the Thousand Islanders. He hated their variety, their vitality and their vigour. So it was his sole aim to take over Thousand Island and get rid of its inhabitants. With enough evil in his red eyes, he had support from the

Samonella Army and the E-Coli Gang. For his general dirty deeds, he had employed the E-Number Crew. They were the least intelligent creatures in existence but useful for odd jobs such as writing letters.

"I hate those goody goody Thousand Islanders. I hate the little ones more!"

A few of the E-Number Crew stood in front of Mr Mould. They looked like scrawny blurs of reds, purples, browns and blues and they spoke in low, nervous voices. Every now and then they moved in an agitated shuffle. They knew they would be in serious trouble if they didn't pay attention to Mr Mould and write the letter for him but they also couldn't stand still.

"Let me help mouldy wouldy?"

Miss Additive was a fiercely excitable counsel to Mr Mould. He planned to marry her soon as she inspired him with her devilishly naughty nature. She sauntered over to him and started reading over his shoulder.

Four hours later, Mr Mould was rubbing his hands and congratulating himself.

"I think it's excellent now! We really should do these ransoms a little more often. So Arti must bring the Silver Spoon to me, then he can have his pesky little half-sister back. To end it, I think the letter should say, 'looking forward to your visit to Mould Island, Yours Fungusly. Mr Mould'."

****

Arti read the letter out to Ginger and Kai again. He had been distraught with worry for the last two days but he was slightly relieved now, knowing Ivy was alive at least. The difficulty of getting her back probably hadn't even hit him yet.

"Perhaps we should call the Thousand Island Authorities?" Kai suggested.

Just as Arti was a natural leader and Ginger a passionate supporter, Kai Lan was the more quiet and cautious member of the group. Kai normally had his nose stuck in a book or spent extra time after school with his Science Teacher, Mr Nut. Unfortunately he was also the clumsiest Thousand Islander most people knew. Bounding through classrooms with his floppy green hair often covering his eyes, he usually had at least one minor accident a day. His clumsiness also extended to his speaking skills. He would often find himself tongue tied and talking nonsense in the midst of a conversation. On this occasion, he was right to feel concerned.

Arti ruffled the full green lobes which built up his wonderful crown of hair. "We can't. They won't want to go to Mould Island. It's been peaceful until now and the authorities won't want to start another war. The only way is for me to do as Mr Mould says. Besides, nobody really cares about the Silver Spoon. It's not like it can cause any harm taking it."

Kai wasn't so sure. The Silver Spoon was not just an ornament to him. It was the only seriously guarded part of Thousand Island and every day, Thousand Islanders from miles away came to sit and pray outside the Spoon, wear smaller ones around their necks for good luck and even get married in front of it.

Despite knowing this, in Arti's mind the mission had been set. He would go to Mould Island with the Silver Spoon and save Ivy himself.

As if she was reading his mind, Ginger stood up.

"You're not doing this alone Arti Choke! We're all coming, or at least I am."

She glared at Kai until he nervously nodded too.

Arti smiled weakly in acceptance. He knew the dangers that lay ahead of him and whether he made it back or not, he had to try. His friends were the only people he could really rely on in this situation. With the action agreed, they instantly became more animated and set about preparing themselves. So much were they distracted, they failed to notice another student lurking behind them who had heard everything.

Mr P Nut was busy making the mixtures for his next science class. Or more like making a mess. He was the only teacher who the students really liked. Probably because he let them run a little riot, let them experiment with all sorts of liquids and potions. He was a little crazy as nuttiness ran in his family and it was pure luck if someone managed to have a normal conversation with him. An intelligent man, he floated between talking in sense and pure babbling nonsense. He was often seen walking to the staff room, muttering under his breath with a quizzical look on his face as if he were questioning the fresh air. It was like nobody else existed. Other times, he was perfectly sociable, witty and balanced. Strange behaviour for a man, who with a small frame and slight features, generally would go unnoticed. Nevertheless, his passion for science could not be questioned, he loved inventing, making things work (which didn't happen very often for him) and, more often than not, making things go a little haywire. He was already daydreaming about winning the Best Invention prize at the Eggscellence Awards, in fact he had pretty much sorted his acceptance speech out.

In the classroom with him for summer classes was Al Mond, Kai's good friend. Al was unusually large for a Mond boy. All the rest of his family members were toned, tanned and pretty trim. But Al was not. Nowhere near. He was the chubbiest, roundest Mond you'll ever meet and he was only ever thinking of his next snack. So here he was, only an hour after lunch and dreaming about food. No wonder he had to spend extra time with Mr Nut – he couldn't concentrate in class!

A knock on the door interrupted his wistful thoughts. It was Christopher Cocoa. Christopher was the son of a very wealthy family in Thousand Island, a family whose descendants were mixed from the pure, innocent community members to the naughty troublemakers who made headlines in the news for all the wrong reasons. Christopher was somewhere in the middle but he was definitely in a very naughty mood today and wanted to spoil something. Having heard the conversation between Arti, Ginger and Kai, Christopher was coming straight to Mr Nut to try and get the gang into trouble, especially Mr Nut's star pupil Kai.

"Sir, could I have a word please?"

Mr Nut, who was pottering under his desk, banged his head against it as he got up and crashed back down nursing a rather quickly forming bump.

"Oh Sir, are you alright?" Christopher ran over to where Mr Nut was with fake concern.

"Yes Christopher, I am fine. Now why's the pie die?"

"I beg your pardon Sir?" Christopher backed away, there was a peculiar look on Mr Nut's face.

"Hickory dickory dock, I need another sock, the clock struck nine, the sock's not mine, hickory dickory dock."

Christopher smiled nervously. The man was a barking mad genius. Maybe he was reminding himself of some formula for some science project or something. You never could tell.

"Sir, I have come to tell you about Arti, Kai and Ginger. They are all up to something."

"Up to something. Up to something."

"Well, it's just that they aren't doing this science project......"

"Honky tonk!" Mr Nut retorted.

"Sir?"

"My feet are red, bumpety bump on my head, the mouse is green, where has it been?"

"Well, I have just been in the courtyard Sir, and well, that's where I heard this conversation. Arti Choke is organising a group of them to go to Mould Island."

"Excellent boy! You have done the right thing telling me. This will be dealt with immediately!"

Christopher smirked at his apparent victory.

"I am going to severely punish them for this, the little rascals. Fancy that! Putting a cat in my shoe! What were they thinking? Cats can't live in shoes. Not my shoes anyway, they smell very, very bad!"

"Sir, I am not sure what you mean. I thought we were talking about Arti."

"Arti? Who's Arti? My brother's brother or my mother's mother?"

"Arti Sir. The whole group of them are going to Mould Island!"

"You boy, are not permitted to go to Mould Island, how many times must I tell you? Especially when you don't have a warm enough jacket. The weather's not great over there at this time of the year."

Christopher sighed. It was useless. There was no getting through to Mr Nut. He was not going to stop them. Al, having heard the whole conversation, left the classroom to find Kai and tell him.

Arti was busy. He had to get the Silver Spoon from the highly guarded Grater Building. It was difficult because it seemed to be so well protected by the small but very efficient Thousand Island Security Team and their high tech equipment. The Grater was a very tall building, with lots of little windows which looked like tiny slits from afar, allowing minimal sight of what was inside. It was made from shiny steel and from a very wide base, it narrowed as it got higher. It had been designed by Professor Broccoli. It wasn't a very pretty building but it wasn't meant to be. It had been built with a purpose. To withstand all forces, natural and unnatural which could damage it. At the top, the Silver Spoon sparkled, stunning the Island with its bright light like a lighthouse.

The area was packed with Islanders coming to pray and tourists visiting. It was so busy, Arti was able to seize his one opportunity.

In a matter of seconds, he had darted across to the maintenance lift which was stationed on the ground floor whilst the cleaner took his break. With all his strength and speed, he began to pull the lift up, quickly rising towards the top of the Grater. He could feel his heart beating hard and sweat running down his face, crazy thoughts racing in his head. He was going to faint. And then suddenly, he was there. He had reached the top!

All that remained now was to grab the Silver Spoon and escape. Well, you could say "all" as if it was only a small task but it was actually going to be extremely difficult. Especially when the cabinet alarm would activate laser guns on the stairs and in lifts, which only the guards were protected against. There was no way of deactivating the alarm, the only way was when all sixteen security chiefs and Mayor Naise locked their individual keys in to the huge security box. On top of that, he had to get his eye lens scanned to check he was authorised to go in. It was never going to be something Arti could have organised well in such a short space of time. He and Ginger had worked out as best a plan as they could. Arti waited for a moment and then with a sigh, walked down the long corridor that led to the Silver Spoon cabinet. At the end hung the cameras and laser guns. From his rucksack, Arti pulled out a large black sheet. It had a hood at the top of it with straps sewn on to the bottom, top and sides of the material. He quickly covered his head with the hood and put his feet and hands through the straps. Then he got down on the black floor, completely stretched on his front and instantly hidden from the cameras. Slowly, he began sliding himself forward.

Arti still had to be slow, the first laser was only slightly above his thick hair and if he came within a millimetre of its ray, he would be the target of a very powerful and deadly weapon. As he shuffled forward, he could see the Spoon glinting. Even though it was less than a foot tall, the sparkle almost blinded Arti! As he lurched forward and picked it up, a sudden violent alarm erupted through the tower.

Amazingly, he had the Silver Spoon in his possession and amazingly, he hadn't been caught by the laser guns. With the unlikelihood of even getting this far, he hadn't planned any further. Now though, the guns were in full action and having nowhere to go, he had been forced into a small room behind the cabinet. Now the guards were all over the top floor, they would get to him soon. He was backed in a corner, clutching the sparkling Silver Spoon. As Arti held it now, he felt a rush of energy coming from it and for such a small object, the Spoon felt incredibly heavy. He looked around the room, desperately seeking something to help him. There was nothing, the room was bare with not even a cupboard to hide in. Arti peered outside the window, careful not to let the big lights that were now circling the tower help the guards see him. People were beginning to crowd round and sirens in the distance suggested the arrival of more officials. Arti rummaged through his rucksack with dwindling hope. He could hear the guards getting closer.

The doors opened and slammed shut with a "clear" being bellowed from one of the guards as they passed through each room. The voice was getting louder, nearing the room Arti was in.

Suddenly, there was a small movement from the side of his bag. Then there was another slight twitch. Curious, Arti slowly unzipped the pocket, expecting an insect to come out and sting him. But something quite the opposite jumped out and started bouncing around the room. It was difficult to work out what it was because it was going completely crazy, springing from the floor to the ceiling in seconds, whizzing side ways and plummeting down so quickly that it was all just a haze. Arti jumped up and tried to follow it around the room, attempting to at least get a glimpse of what it was. The sight was quite amusing and if Arti had not been in such a dangerous and difficult situation, he might have even laughed at the sight of himself chasing this unknown creature.

"Stop!" he ordered.

But it just carried on zipping around Arti.

Arti couldn't understand what this strange, energetic thing was. It reminded him of Ivy, of her excitement. He was sure Ivy would love this thing. Then he suddenly realised. Of course, it was Kazai! Ivy's little pet! Nobody but Ivy could have such a lively little pet.

"Kazai, stop now! If you ever want to see Ivy again, you'll do exactly as I say!"

Below the tower, there was a growing crowd who had witnessed the alarm being activated and could see the security lights flashing. Islanders shoved past each other, the excitement and intrigue buzzing in their conversations as they wondered what was happening at the top.

The door swung open and several guards piled in. A few Courgettes, Carrots and Chief Tom Ato. Arti was right in front of them, standing on the window sill. The window was open with lights swooping and sirens blaring from outside.

"Right mister" Chief Ato said, "you've got the whole town running after you, disrupting the nice quiet life we have here. You've got yourself into big trouble. Walk out with us quietly and we won't force you."

A Carrot Cavalier chipped in.

"Like anyone could get away now, we've got the little culprit completely cornered now."

He laughed loudly. Soon, they were all laughing at Arti.

"I haven't stolen the Silver Spoon for my pleasure. I need it to help someone else. I can't tell you anymore than that but I need you to trust me and let me go. I promise I will come back with the Silver Spoon once I have sorted everything out."

The group stopped to listen to him but then burst out into laughter again. A few of them began edging closer to Arti.

"Well, I did ask nicely."

As the guard tried to grab Arti, the rucksack was yanked and Arti was snatched from the window sill and out into the air. He was held by the firm grasp of Kazai who had stretched himself to a tree in the forest and was swiftly sailing towards it. Kazai clung to the tree and Arti with all his might. His purple face was darkening with the strain and he was almost out of energy but the memory of Ivy kept him going.

The horrified guards ran out of the room, some waiting for the lift, some running down the stairs in panic, all of them on their radios. Below, the speed of Arti's flight meant that he wasn't really noticed by any observers and even if someone had seen him, they would have hardly believed their eyes.

With Kai, Ginger and Arti reunited, it took the three of them some time to relay their stories to each other, it was sheer excitement knowing they had managed to get through so much already. Arti displayed the Silver Spoon and they all held it in turn, amazed by its shine, weight and the strange sensation they got from it. However, it was not long before Arti took control of the plan again. He had decided that the quickest way to Mould Island would be to cross the Mineral Lakes, into the Fizzy Sea and straight to Mould Island. It was also the most dangerous. The Fizzy Sea was really wild and stormy, Thousand Islanders never crossed it. But it was the only way to reach Ivy quickly. The three Islanders now needed a boat. It had to be strong and able to withstand the turbulence of the sea. Kai and Ginger had been busy in preparation.

"We went to the human wastelands and found lots" Ginger enthused. "I found this great margarine tub which could work for the boat base, crisp packet for the sail and wood for the wheels. And I've got this cling film to give us cover."

"You mean 'we'" Kai piped, looking a little disgruntled. He had found most of the equipment and given Ginger different ideas for their uses.

"C'mon, let's get building" Arti instructed as he winked at Kai, knowing full well that he had done all the work.

It was quite late by the time they had finished making the boat which they named the Big Cheese. They were all tired from their hard work but it did look magnificent and they were proud of it. After a late dinner, they decided to get some sleep and start their journey in the early hours of the morning. With a sense of satisfaction, they all made their way to their sleeping bags.

According to the updates on Kai's radio, the search for the invaders of the Grater had moved back into the main town of Thousand Island. Security believed the culprits were local kids so now all houses were being searched, which meant they were safe for now.

As the sun rose in the early hours of the morning, just as the birds were chirping excitedly and discussing the day's weather forecast, Ginger and Kai were woken by a large banging noise. It was Arti hitting the side of the tub with a branch of a tree. It was the wake up call.

"Rise and shine! We have a long day ahead of us!"

The lakes were sparkling. It was like there were tiny diamonds in the water, the whole lake was glittering. The shimmering sheet was vast and went far out in the distance before it joined the Fizzy Sea. In the distance, the outline of the mountains which led to Mould Island was slight but still visible enough to tower threateningly at them.

The Blue Cheese was ready for her big debut. The group cleaned their sleeping area, packed everything they didn't need in boxes, strapped them down and released the sail. In the morning sunshine, the boat looked grand and beautiful. They began rolling it down to the lake and with its large wooden wheels, the tub moved with ease. Ginger and Kai who had been pushing from the back felt the weight of the boat release onto the water and jumped aboard to join Arti. A big cheer rang around the boat as it sailed forward. For most of the day, they had quite a tranquil journey, sailing along comfortably on the Mineral Lakes. The breeze whistled around them disturbed only by Ginger's outbursts of instructions or excitable singing. It was only as the sun began to settle, the sky grew darker and the boat began to rock, that a sense of fear clouded over them. They all knew that they were entering the Fizzy Sea now and the nice, relaxing journey would be no more. They were right to believe so. All at once, great big waves came crashing against the Blue Cheese, spraying the boat with white foam. They were thrust violently from side to side and knocked into each other in the darkness. Overhead, a storm began to brew with flashes of lightning stinging the sea and low rumbles of thunder teasing the sky. They were all soaked, with rain gushing down on them and every now and then a wave sweeping over them. It was difficult for Arti to guide the group as he couldn't even see in the distance, he had no idea where they were. From being in the calm tranquillity and sunlight of the lake, they were now engulfed in complete darkness and the terror of the tides.

"Guys, there's no way we're going to stay on board and control the Blue Cheese. The sea is far too stormy. We can't afford to lose each other." Arti had to shout against the menacing sea as they all held on to the side of the boat, afraid of being swept in. "It's best we go down and strap ourselves in our sleeping bags, it's the only chance we have of surviving through the night."

As soon as the words left Arti's mouth, Kai bolted down to strap himself in, covering even his head with the blanket in fear. Ginger and Arti were soon strapped in beside him. They were tired, wet and scared and none of them had the strength to work against the wrath of the sea. As the thunder growled outside, the rain and stormy sea crashed against the boat viciously. Clutching hard to their sleeping bags, the group anxiously lay in silence, praying to make it through the night.

"You're bad and naughty and my brother is going to severely punish you when he gets here!"

Ivy was telling her keeper, Stinky Chink what a bad monster he was. Stinky Chink was Mr Mould's pet. The dragon like beast weighed two hundred times what Ivy did, could fire blazing flames from his nostrils and could beat half an army down with the swing of his tail. His most dangerous weapon, though, was his smell. Stinky Chink had not bathed for three hundred years. So his natural smell was a cross between cow dung and dog's breath. Hence the sweet, lovable name of Stinky Chink. In the past, any traitors or enemies of Mr Mould had been banished to his cell. The prisoners would die a slow and painful death from inhaling the toxic smell of Stinky Chink. His current record was poor Mrs Cracker who fainted in fifteen days. He did also have the ability to smoke hostages to death with the flames he fired out but it had been so long since his owner had offered him a target, there was much doubt that Stinky Chink could still perform. Mr Mould had planned for Ivy to reside with Stinky Chink until her brother delivered what he had demanded. If Arti didn't turn up in time, or if he tried to be silly and get the authorities involved, Stinky Chink would finish Ivy off without needing any help.

Stinky Chink roared and blasted flames of fire from his nostrils in Ivy's direction most of the day. His reputation would be in tatters if he was seen to be getting told off by a little girl not even the size of his left nostril. Ivy waved the smoke away from her eyes. The stench of Stinky Chink was beginning to weaken her but she still seemed to have the energy to nag him.

"Do you realise how much you could put your fire to good use? You would have so much fun lighting up everyone's barbeques for them in the summer, helping to get the hot air balloons to rise and heating the whole island in the winter. Your job's so boring too! Don't you ever get bored of being on your own with nobody to talk to and nobody to love you?"

Stinky Chink threw some red flashes towards Ivy. He actually missed the peace he had before. Why couldn't she just keep quiet and beg for him not to hurt her like all his previous prisoners?

Instead, she moaned about the interior of his dungeon, the lighting in the room, the space in her cell and the mess around her.

"My mother would never let us live like this, how can you even think clearly?"

And it went on and on and on. Stinky Chink wondered if it was at all possible to die a death from someone ranting at you. That was probably a slow and painful death. This was not good. Maybe it was time for phase two. He mustered up all his strength (it had been a while since he had had to be so forceful) and lifted his tail in the air. With a little bit of sashaying for a dramatic effect and a roar for sound, Stinky Chink smashed his tail down very close to Ivy's cell. The whole dungeon rocked. Ivy screamed and jumped back into the corner. Stinky Chink smiled with satisfaction. He was pleased with himself for not having lost his touch. Maybe he could enjoy some silence now.

"My brother's going to save me from you, you mean, mean animal" Ivy sobbed.

****

With school finished, Mr Nut was busy with his new invention. It was unlikely that anyone could tell what it was. Metal rods were poking out from one end of a large wooden box. Pink and purple feathers were stuck on another side and there was a propeller at the front. Wheels were fixed at the bottom but of all different sizes so the actual box stood lopsided. But Mr Nut seemed very excited with it, muttering away and congratulating himself on his apparent success.

"That's the one, go go Nutty."

Mr Nut's nickname when he was younger had been 'Nutty' and he continued to keep up the tradition even if it did mean he was talking to himself.

"If we just move this screw over here then..."

Suddenly the box collapsed! Fortunately, in true Nut fashion, it collapsed in style. Firstly the rods fell off. Then the wheels rolled away in different directions. Then the wooden sides fell one by one. And for the finale, the feathers were blown abruptly into the air by all the commotion and drifted back to the floor one by one. Mr Nut was sat cross legged in the middle, surrounded by the remains of the catastrophic crash, with the pink and purple feathers drifting around him. He seemed to be in deep thought. Then he started muttering. He quickly jumped up, ran over to his note book and started scribbling away furiously in a strange language.

"And moving the illecuous to the bystacker, with the forandaga looped over will ensure a more sturdy cantakalous."

At that point, there was a knock on the door. It was Al Mond. Al had been standing there a while but could not bring himself to disturb what seemed like a very important moment to Mr Nut.

"Al, my boy, come in." Mr Nut pulled up a chair for Al and leaned on the desk himself, with two feathers now stuck to the top of his head. Al sat and stared at the two objects settled on Mr Nut's head, wondering how he should tell his teacher. Mr Nut realised their presence and quickly removed them, deciding to use the end of one to clean his ears. Al was a little disgusted but not really surprised.

"I need some help Al, are you up to it or have you grain in the brain? I tell you someone who would know what to do. Clever little Kai! He'll know it all. In fact, let's get uppity up and see him now, I'm sure he's already bored with summer holidays."

Al jumped out of his seat. "Oh no Sir" he protested, "we can't go to see him."

Mr Nut ignored him. "Al, Pal, you must go and rest your little head now while I go and see Kai."

"Sir, you can't go and see him, you can't." But Mr Nut was already walking towards the door mumbling to himself.

"Sir, please, sir. You can't go, there's a big reason, you can't."

Mr Nut stopped.

"Why not?"

"Because" Al paused. "Because, he's on his way to Mould Island!"

It was coming up to midday now and the violence of the Fizzy Sea had dissolved into the depths of the water, bubbling away and waiting to erupt again with the arrival of the evening. The waves now gently rocked against each other as if in slumber, with the blues, greens and white spray all merging in one. The Blue Cheese was no longer afloat, the Fizzy Sea had ejected it out of its waters and it was now stationed on some rocks, locked into an immovable position. The sail had been ripped apart and debris lay across the rocks and over the boat. The oars had been dislodged and now floated miles away from each other in the sea, making their journeys to other destinations. The tub had cracked at points and water was seeping in and out.

A little distance from the boat, the water met a small sandy cave. Here lay Arti, Ginger and Kai – all quite knocked out from what must have been a tumultuous ride, all drying out from the drenching the sea had dealt them. They had been sleeping for quite some time now. The sun in the distance peeked into the darkness of the cove, running its rays over them one by one. Although the beam did not affect Ginger and Kai, it caused Arti to stir.

Suddenly he jerked and woke with a start, calling for Ivy. The others instantly woke and ran over to him.

"Arti, you ok?" Ginger checked.

Arti, having had a moment to bring himself back to reality, immediately stood up and looked around.

"Where are we?" He walked out of the cave, with the sea just swaying at his feet, and the sand pulling away with the soft waves. Arti reviewed the Blue Cheese a few metres away from them. It had surprisingly held out well he thought, at least they were alive. But where were they? It did not look like the Mould Island he had researched.

He pulled out his map. After a few minutes of inspection, he smiled.

"Guys, we've actually taken a different route and somehow, through the torrential rain and sea we've ended up right on Mould Island, with the Fungi Forest just on the side of the mountains here. We've got here sooner than we thought!"

****

Miss Additive was standing in front of the full length mirror, sashaying in her new black dress. It was tight from the top, snaked snugly on her hips then flared out with strands of black falling in all directions. It was her outfit to celebrate her engagement with Mr Mould. For a long time he had been pestering her and eventually she had relented.

"So how do I look?" Miss Additive purred, expecting a whole half hour of compliments. Mr Mould sat in his armchair, grunting and pulling wax from his ears.

"Great Mrs Mould to be!" he said without looking up. "Mrs Mould, do you know how lucky you are going to be, sharing such a great name. You must be so excited to marry me!"

This was not the response Miss Additive was expecting. In fact she felt disgusted by her fiancé. But this was not the time to reveal her real plans, she didn't care as long as she was spoilt rotten and shared Mr Mould's power. She flicked her hair, applied her lipstick and then with a wicked smile, held Mr Mould's hand and entered the ballroom.

As the couple did not have any friends or family, the E-Coli Gang had been invited as guests to their party and the E-Number Crew were ordered to entertain. They banged away on steel drums as Miss Additive and Mr Mould gorged on different specialities of fat and fungus filled nibbles. The room had been half decorated – there were weeds and twigs twisted together to form banners and "Congratulations" glistened in mud on the walls. The E-Coli Gang and the E-Number Crew tried to mingle with each other but as this was also their first real social event, they were quite unsure how to behave. Finally, after an hour or so of banging away on the drums, the E-Number Crew stopped and made their way to the middle of the room.

E 131 stepped forward. He was midnight blue, top to toe, so thin and long that if he stood sideways he would disappear. But he still had a hungry menace in his red eyes.

"For your entertainment tonight, we are going to perform a traditional E-Number dance. It's called The Hyper."

The group split into three rows of five and after a short silence to build the tension, the drummers began to play. The first row started jumping side to side, the middle row started jumping front to back and the back row jumped on the spot. Then they all jumped outwards until a circle started forming. Once the circle had constructed itself, the dancers started running, following the shape of the circle and shouting as they went. The shouting had no rhythm, no synchronisation or any comprehendible lyrics. It really was just shouting. Over each other. And it got louder and louder. And they started running faster, trying to catch up with the person ahead of them, trying to run away from whoever was behind them. Then suddenly they fell out of formation and were just running in all directions, bumping into each other, falling over each other, still shouting. Then one member got on the floor and started rolling around, with the rest of them following the action. Suddenly there were reds, blues, greens, yellows all over the floor, rolling around and still yelling. Mr Mould seemed to enjoy the performance, Miss Additive was less impressed. Several times, she covered her ears from the noise and reminded herself that this show thankfully would end at some point soon. She looked over to Mr Mould, knowing she would share his power soon and looking forward to the chance to control the land. She was already wondering how she would get rid of the husband she was about to marry.

CHAPTER

8

The Fungi Forest looked dense and dark. Above the twisted, tall trees, a mist had formed, bringing with it a damp odour. Arti scanned the area with a sense of unease. Ginger and Kai stood there, motionless. The excitement had subdued into fear although nobody wanted to admit it. Arti sensed his friends' anxiety.

"Ok, well it looks a little dark."

"Much more eerie and about ten times more dangerous than home" Kai volunteered, not being able to help himself.

Arti shot him a look. Kai was not helping in the slightest bit.

"Let's just go for it guys" Arti said boldly and took the first step into the forest. Ginger and Kai switched on their torches and followed Arti.

Inside the forest, the trees were lined with furry layers of mould. The ground was rolling with large circles of bacterial growth, with swirls of purples, browns and greens inside them. As well as marking their presence on the floor, the disgusting discs also draped from several trees, swaying like curtains in the icy wind. Arti, Ginger and Kai did their best to avoid them but as the wind pushed the hanging mould in their direction, they found themselves bumping into each other clumsily. Suddenly a line of arrows darted over their heads.

"What was that?" Arti exclaimed, spinning around. Suddenly a dozen more flew towards them.

"Run!" Arti ordered. "Find somewhere to hide." And it was the only thing they could do. Behind them, hundreds of the E-Coli Gang were coming after them, with hundreds of more arrows too. They looked menacing, their long, black bodies, fuzzy and gaunt hovering towards the group like grim ghosts. They were light and speedy, swarming fast and furious towards the terrified three. Every time Arti looked behind, he could see this big mass of black coming towards them. They seemed to multiply and the forest darkened even more. Soon, Arti thought, they would be engulfed in this blackness, they had no chance really. There seemed to be no end to the trees, the mould and the darkness.

"What about throwing rocks at them?" Ginger suggested, almost out of breath and hope.

"That's not going to help at all" Kai objected.

She took a chance anyway and launched a few rocks in the direction of the advancing enemy. But she watched in dismay as the rocks hurtled through the E-Coli gang, making no impact on them at all. The black clouds were getting closer with their evil shrills ringing harder. Suddenly, a few of the E-Coli Gang let out cries of terror and fizzled away. One of the rocks Ginger had thrown pushed through a leaf allowing the light from the sun to fall on to them. With the forest being completely covered and no natural light being able to come through at all, it appeared that the E-Coli Gang were only accustomed and able to survive in the dark, dense forest conditions.

"Quick!" Arti instructed "point your torches to them, on the highest light setting!"

The team acted quickly and soon the E-Coli Gang were being stung by the intense light and vanishing like puffs of smoke. Their screams sounded like sharp sirens, echoing all round the forest. They were reduced to less than half of what they started with in a matter of minutes. In all the commotion, the Silver Spoon had also fallen out and it alone brightened the whole forest, making the remaining enemies dissolve away. Such was its strength, even the dying trees seemed to rejuvenate by its sparkle. Arti wondered if he had underestimated the power of the Silver Spoon and what would happen if Mr Mould did have it. For now it didn't matter. The Thousand Island Heroes had survived.

CHAPTER

9

Ivy opened her eyes and yawned. "Mum, I'm ready for school." She got up, still a little sleepy and walked towards the bathroom. Suddenly, she bumped into something hard. Rubbing her eyes, she looked to see what had obstructed her. Probably something she or her brother had forgotten to put away yesterday. But it wasn't anything like that. It was a steel bar. With several others around her. She could feel the floor was cold now. Grey stone instead of her orange bedroom carpet. Peering through the bars, she could see nothing but complete darkness. Then she saw the two red, menacing eyes fixed on her from a distance. She screamed and fell back, realising where she was again. This happened quite frequently now. She would fall asleep and be transformed back home with her loved ones in her dreams and then suddenly wake up to the harsh reality of being captured by Mr Mould and being locked away in this horrible, grotty cell with a vicious beast watching her every move. She burst into tears.

The red eyes advanced towards her and suddenly she was staring at the ugly head of Stinky Chink.

"Oh god, it's you again. Why can't you leave me alone?"

Ivy wondered if there was some way of communicating with the monster without being burnt alive. How could she convince him to change his ways? She remembered her mother used to make up poems to encourage her to finish her dinner. Ivy wasn't very good with poetry but perhaps it was worth a try.

"Stinky Chink has not always been naughty."

Stinky Chink raised his eyebrows.

"Stinky Chink has not always been naughty, that's because he's um, because he's um, um…"

Stinky Chink roared and fired a big flame inches away from Ivy. Then he triumphantly turned and began moving away.

"No, no wait!" Ivy cried out "I haven't finished yet."

"Stinky Chink, um um, Stinky Chink, you aren't so bad, you are just a poor creature who is sad."

Stinky Chink stopped. But he didn't turn around.

"The sun and the wind are both different to me. But they still manage to live in perfect harmony."

He turned around this time.

"My name's Ivy and Thousand Island's my home, I'm sure Stinky had somewhere he loved to roam."

Stinky Chink suddenly had a funny expression on his face. It was something Ivy had never seen him do before. It was a smile!

The gang had arrived to a large, murky swamp. An awful stench hit them immediately and they all groaned in disgust.

"What is that?" Ginger said in a muffled voice as she tried to cover her mouth so as not to consume the smell fully.

"I don't know" Arti replied, feeling rather sick himself.

"Smells kind of familiar to me, quite homely" Kai said quite happily.

Kai quickly realised from Ginger's look of disgust that he had perhaps not explained himself very well. Suddenly it clicked.

"Of course!" he exclaimed. "It's when the eggs are unwell, when they've been attacked by the Salmonella Snakes. They start to smell bad."

"But what would they be doing here?" Ginger knew he was right, Kai always paid attention in Mr Nut's Science class.

"It's so deadly quiet" Arti whispered, having spent the last few minutes scanning through the veils of grey mist and checking for any movement in the foggy waters. "There doesn't seem to be anything here."

"Look there!" Kai suddenly shouted. Something was bobbing along in the water. Arti flashed his torch over it. It was part of an eggshell! Suddenly he could see at least twenty!

"You must be right Kai" Arti said. "These shells must be the remains of the diseased eggs brought here by the Salmonella Snakes. Perhaps we could use the eggshells as stepping stones to get across. We can't walk around and I think the water's too polluted for us to swim in."

"No other way?" Kai checked. He wished the Thousand Island officials were with them, like a proper military operation, with fewer risks than the ones they had taken. He also wished he was back at school, in the comfort of the library and all his wonderful books.

"I'm sorry" Arti apologised.

"C'mon then" Ginger said in encouragement, "it might actually be fun."

Kai rolled his eyes. He knew this was going to be anything but fun. Arti, however, didn't hesitate. He jumped on to a shell and quickly on to the next. He was advancing fast. Suddenly the water seemed to ripple. Then there were waves and a long and scaly creature jumped out from under a shell. Far from pretty, it was a dirty dark brown and purple colour, with huge, evil, green eyes and a long mouth baring razor sharp teeth.

"Move Arti!" Ginger screamed. The vicious creature snapped the shell in its mouth just as Arti had managed to jump on to another shell. It was close!

"That must be a Salmonella Snake!" Ginger screamed as Arti rushed forward across the swamp. "We've got no chance of crossing the water without them snapping us up!"

"You can do it guys" Arti shouted now standing on the other side and in one piece.

Kai looked nervously at Ginger who was equally unhappy about the position they were in. Then Kai looked back and trembled at the thought of meeting more of the E-Coli Gang who would be very angry by now. There was no other choice and with a sigh he leapt forward surprising himself and Ginger as he skated across.

"I didn't know it was a race but I'm certainly not coming last!" Ginger announced as she quickly followed.

"Don't look behind!" Arti ordered as three shadows came to the water's surface and suddenly more Salmonella Snakes soared out, saw like teeth snapping the shells Ginger and Kai had just been positioned on. Whether it was their fear or pure madness, Arti thought he had never seen his friends move so fast and was truly grateful when they finally made it to him. He rushed to hug them and was about to congratulate them on their bravery when suddenly they were whipped up and captured in a net.

"So close, what a shame!"

Miss Additive was smiling at them teasingly from below as they hung, helplessly from the tree.

CHAPTER

Forgotten about Al and Mr Nut? Well they had certainly not forgotten about their fellow Thousand Islanders making their way through Mould Island to rescue Ivy. In the old gym area on the morning of a school holiday, Mr Nut was banging away, throwing pieces of metal around and pressing the buttons of several very loud machines. This was all while being dressed in a purple tracksuit with a pink cape that was printed with yellow daisies. He also wore a big cowboy hat with multi-coloured streamers dangling from the top and tennis balls stuck to the brim. Al plucked up courage to ask why there were tennis balls stuck to the top of the hat. In fact he had wanted to question the whole outfit but he started with the hat. Mr Nut replied immediately, as if the answer was obvious.

"My brain is a very sensitive thing. I must keep it covered at all costs. Tennis balls defend the brain."

With an answer like that, Al decided not to bother asking any more questions.

It was still very early in the morning and Mr Nut was proud of how much he had done. He had decided with Al that they would fly over to Mould Island themselves and save the others. Mr Nut had also declared he would build the most advanced flying machine to transport them there and although his current activity was a little peculiar, he assured Al that he was indeed building an aircraft. Al had spent the whole morning watching Mr Nut 6.38 metres away.

"You must stay 6.38 metres away" Mr Nut had insisted, "there is serious risk to my vehicle and to your safety if you come any closer." So, for the entire morning, Al was poised in one position, watching his fairly mad teacher banging away at his invention. To his relief, it was only a few hours until he was able to move again.

"I am not quite sure I have the part I need Al. How about we take a trip to the parts store?"

Al jumped at the opportunity to get out and they were soon seated in Mr Nut's vehicle, the butter dish. Long and rectangular, the butter dish was made from stainless steel. It was a classic. The front and back were defined by ledges which dipped in to make the passenger compartment. There was no need to control it with a steering wheel, the driver only had to stretch his right arm out in the direction he wanted to travel. To move faster, he only had to move his left arm higher. Not surprisingly, Mr Nut's left arm started completely vertical. The butter dish was so fast, it was like gliding on ice. The trees, buildings, sky, all seemed to merge into one as they sped down the roads with Mr Nut urging the dish to go faster. Al, however, felt that any faster and his already green shaded face might turn purple and he might be sick. He thought he must be going mad too as they passed what he was sure was the general parts store.

"Mr Nut" he bellowed over the wind and engine roar, "did we not just past the store?"

"No Al, whatever are you talking about, we're just coming up to it on our left."

Suddenly Mr Nut swerved to his left and with Al holding on for dear life, drove down a small hill. Al could not see any store in sight and they were still driving at full speed. All he could see was a big oak tree. And Mr Nut was driving towards the tree with no signs of slowing down or changing direction.

"Urm, Mr Nut, we're heading towards a tree!"

"You've finally got it!" Mr Nut exclaimed, circling his left arm to accelerate even further. Above Al's screams, he congratulated the good traffic conditions and the quiet roads. They were almost at the tree now, travelling at an incredible speed. Al covered his eyes. Just as he peeked, he saw the strong pillar of bark seconds away from them and just as he contemplated jumping out, the trunk of the tree opened up and the butter dish flew inside. They surged forward and were suddenly spiralling down. Then all of a sudden, the dish ground to a halt. They were in complete darkness. Mr Nut clapped his hands twice. Lights filled the room and Al was amazed with what he saw. They were in a huge warehouse deep down in the tree. Hung all around them were building materials, equipment and machines. Everything was labelled and stored neatly.

"I'll be with you in a moment Mr Nut" a voice said from behind some shelves.

"No problems, I'll just take a wander" Mr Nut replied, in a surprisingly controlled voice. "Come, I'll show you a few things" he said to Al.

They walked over to one side of the room. Leaning against a wall, stood a huge circular object, with a raised ring in the middle. It seemed to be made of something similar to what Al thought they used in pottery but he wasn't sure.

"What is that?"

"That" Mr Nut stated quite proudly, "is the flying saucer. It was built years ago in the days when we fought the likes of Mr Mould and the evils which now inhabit Mould Island. It was used to travel through air. You could carry more than fifty Thousand Island soldiers on it."

"What about this?" Al asked, pleased with the one and only normal response he had just got from Mr Nut. He was pointing to a long object with three prongs on its head.

"Oh, the fork fighter, oh that's a story now isn't it. The fork fighter used to be attached to the front of any of our vehicles and when the enemy were close by the fork fighter would be pulled back and catapulted in the direction of the enemy which it usually trapped with its prongs." Mr Nut was smiling.

"You're acting like all the fighting was an enjoyable experience" Al challenged, annoyed that his teacher might actually be condoning violence.

"Not at all" Mr Mould protested. "In fact, the reason why Mr Mould has control of that island is purely because the Thousand Islanders retreated, they all wanted the battling to stop. Everyone was tired with the fighting and really, it isn't in our nature. Although some of us get lured by trouble. I remember a good friend who lost herself in Mr Mould's wicked ways. She was so good and sweet but also hungry for attention and power. What fun we used to have! We spent many days talking, laughing and dancing! But one day I saw the effect she had had on some poor soldier. He was hyperactive and uncontrollably in love with her, Mr Mould had encouraged her to bewitch him.

When she realised what she had done, she broke down into tears and the next day she just disappeared."

Mr Nut looked reflective and was probably the most still and stable Al had seen him the whole time he had known him. Just then a bulky figure stepped out to meet them. He was large on top and skinnier as his body went down, shaped like a curved V with smooth, bright red skin.

"Mr Nut, welcome!"

"Hello Sergeant Pepper! This is Al, one of my students helping me out today."

"Welcome son" Sergeant Pepper spoke authoritatively. He stared at Al as if he were capturing a photo of him. "This is a private warehouse, unknown to many, You'll keep it that way."

Al knew this wasn't a question. He felt slightly scared.

As if he could read his mind, Sergeant Pepper's face softened and he smiled.

"Well then, let's get you some parts!"

A few hours later, the butter dish was laden with boxes. As they waved goodbye to Sergeant Pepper, Mr Nut resumed his eccentric behaviour including his crazy driving. But for Al, his opinion of his teacher had changed. Somewhere under all that craziness was actually a very intelligent man.

When they returned to the school, Mr Nut enthusiastically resumed his work with his new parts with Al 6.38 metres away again. An hour later, Mr Nut shouted in jubilation.

"Al, I'm all done! Here it goes!"

The engine began whirring and the propeller began circling. Al held his breath with excitement. There seemed to be a little movement when suddenly the engine ground to a halt and the propeller flew off its position, into the air and came crashing down to the floor in bits. Then, the sides of the aircraft collapsed. All that was left was Mr Nut in his pink, daisy covered cape.

"I can't believe it!" Mr Nut despaired and proceeded to kick the rest of the aircraft so that after a few minutes and a great deal of energy from the irritated teacher, all that remained was a pile of rubble.

CHAPTER

The Thousand Islanders had been tied up in Mould Castle. Miss Additive was trying to convince them to hand over the Silver Spoon which Arti had firmly in his possession and leave quietly. She preferred not to hurt anyone and besides, the E-Number Crew were far from violent even if they looked dangerous. Arti had refused to leave without Ivy who Miss Additive couldn't get to without Mr Mould finding out.

"Well, let's see" she hissed in annoyance, "maybe there is another way of making you see sense."

She clicked her fingers and suddenly E 104 and E 131 of the E-Number Crew were standing in front of them. They were dressed in baggy jeans, almost rolling off their wispy hips and big gold medallions hung from their necks. E 104 was a bright yellow colour and twitched continuously. He seemed a lot less scary than his tall, darker partner.

"Off you go boys" Miss Additive ordered, as she sat back into her big jewel encrusted chair. The two members of the E-Number Crew did a countdown from three and suddenly jumped into action. Swaying slightly, they began rapping:

E 104:   Hey Arti, Farty, pudding and pie
          You gotta give in now or you might just die
          That Silver Spoon is all we need
          Hand it over and you'll be freed

E 131:   It's only a Silver Spoon and it'll be kept well
          Away from Mr Mould who would make it hell
          Miss Additive just wants to be a good queen
          Be nice to her kingdom, never be mean

Both together: Hand it over, hand it over, the Silver Spoon,
          hand it over
          Take it, take it, freedom and safety, take it

E 104:   One gem, two gem, three gem, four
          We just want the Silver Spoon and promise no more
          Don't deny Miss Additive, you'll just lose
          Better to be safe, play by her rules

E 131:   Miss Additive will win and control them all
          She'll even make Mr Mould fall
          Don't be foolish, use your brain,
          Don't make us have to cause you pain

Both together: Hand it over, hand it over, the Silver Spoon,
          hand it over
          Take it, take it, freedom and safety, take it

Throughout the rap, E 104 and E 131 rocked from side to side, pointing their long, bony fingers in Arti's direction and nodding with their lines. When they had finished, they slapped each others hands, and started talking in their own made up language which they thought sounded cool.

"You know bro, that was ghetto gilded."

"Yeh man, I'm down with that, we knows what turkey we's got."

"Yes, thank you boys" Miss Additive sighed "not sure what turkeys have to do with it but your vocal skills are quite something. So Arti" she purred "what have you decided?"

Before Arti could reply, the door swung open and Mr Mould entered.

"I hope you weren't thinking of having a party without me!"

Miss Additive had been caught out. The E-Coli Gang followed after Mr Mould and quickly tied Miss Additive and her E-Number Crew up. She looked far from happy now she was tied up and on the grimy floor. It was spoiling her hair, make up and her whole regal image. She attempted her most alluring, pleading face for Mr Mould which he instantly dismissed. He looked at her with almost as much disgust as she regarded for him. They were obviously not the perfect match he had previously thought.

"Unfortunately little miss vain is going to have to get used to this treatment. I know exactly what you have been up to. I really don't think that's a great basis for marriage. You're useless to me. Not good enough for Thousand Island and not nearly bad enough for Mould Island. Must be a terrible feeling not having a place to call home."

Miss Additive thought to profess even more artificial love for him but the thought made her sick and she did have some pride. No amount of long black dresses could make up for how much she despised him and she now deeply regretted not helping the young group who had come with honest intentions of helping others out.

"You are quite possibly the most hideous thing I have seen" she retorted.

Mr Mould yawned and turned his attention to the Thousand Islanders.

"It was stupid to enter Mould Island. It was stupid to think you could make it into my castle and leave alive. To think that bringing the Silver Spoon would guarantee anything but suffering for you. But then I guess you have the silly notions of love, compassion and loyalty. I think that believing in such things is even more stupid than your actions so far. To make this long trip for one girl. One very annoying girl I should say."

Arti glared at him. He did not shake or quiver like the others at the pain that was about to greet them. Fixing his eyes vehemently on Mr Mould, he suddenly burst into life.

"We might all die but we have the goodness in our hearts to die fighting for what is right. Ginger, Kai, you're both the best friends anyone could ever have. I brought you all onto this mission and I am sorry I couldn't save Ivy or you. But we can try to save our friends and family in Thousand Island. We should not give up till the very end. Miss Additive, you have a far bigger strength than your beauty. Somewhere you have a strong, deep heart. Let's not do ourselves injustice and let our enemies have our courage so easily."

Miss Additive was amazed at how someone so much younger than her could talk so much sense. Ginger and Kai seemed to have forgotten their imminent death, touched by his brave words. Raising his voice higher, Arti commanded "fight with me!"

As if an alarm had been raised and electric currents had charged through them, they were all suddenly fighting with the vines that held them back and gnawing at each others in an attempt to free themselves. Miss Additive, unconcerned by how ridiculous she looked now, wriggled closer to join them.

Mr Mould, now bored with all the righteous talk decided it was time to get rid of them all. With a clap of his hands, the E-Coli Gang began to assemble together, spinning individually then clustering in twos, then fours, then eights until they were all one violent tornado. In the depths of black, flashes of red shot through as their evil eyes penetrated their victims, getting ready to pounce. The room became deathly dark and even shook. Mr Mould placed himself on a fungus decorated chair with the Silver Spoon he had forced from Arti now on his lap. He was ready to watch every single one of the do-gooders annihilated as they had caused him enough trouble.

The room started shaking more violently. The floorboards were creaking up. Suddenly Mr Mould was thrown off his chair. There seemed to be something shaking the floor from beneath them and it didn't appear to be the E-Coli Gang.

At that moment, the floorboards crashed apart as Stinky Chink's head bashed through.

The E-Coli tornado was swept aside. Soon Stinky Chink was fully in the room, his head almost touching the ceiling and his tail beating down below him. He looked rather angry too. But then Arti noticed something in Stinky Chink's left ear. Just sitting there. It was...

"Ivy!" Arti exclaimed.

"Arti! I thought you might need a little help, didn't look like you were going to make it to me any time soon!"

She was still as cheeky as ever. But he loved it. And Arti made a mental note never to complain about her again if they ever made it out of Mould Island. Having been thrown into a corner, Mr Mould was not pleased.

"Stinky Chink! I order you to kill all these stupid Thousand Islanders, including the one stuck in your ear. Now!"

Stinky Chink lifted his head high and then dived straight back down, his angry face hurtling towards Mr Mould. His head was level with Mr Mould now and with a deep breath, he responded to Mr Mould with an almighty roar. The walls behind Mr Mould collapsed out and Mr Mould had to hold on just to stop himself from falling out too. It was clear Stinky Chink's priorities had changed.

"I told you not to be so mean" Ivy scolded "bad things happen to those who are bad."

Stinky Chink nodded and almost looked sweet and lovable as Ivy stroked his ear. Then his usual menacing expression returned.

"No, no, c'mon now Stinky Chink, I'll get you a nice big dungeon, how about that?" reasoned Mr Mould.

Stinky Chink did not seem interested in negotiating and instead took a deep breath, getting ready to spray Mr Mould with the poison that could destroy him. Just then, Ginger screamed. The E-Coli Gang were surrounding her, not wasting any time now.

"Stinky, we need to help Ginger!" Ivy ordered.

The once loyal pet of Mr Mould turned his attention to the E-Coli Gang, spraying them with his stinky poison. They recoiled in pain and began disappearing. In the meantime, the rest of the group freed themselves and chased Mr Mould who had escaped and still had the Silver Spoon.

"Hurry guys, we can't let him get away now."

Arti was renewed with life again. Knowing Ivy was safe, his mind was clear and he could concentrate on getting the pride of Thousand Island back.

Miss Additive had stayed behind with Ivy, ensuring that Stinky Chink was able to exterminate all the rest of the E-Coli Gang and all of Mr Mould's remaining weapons. She had taken on a brand new role, goodness and a sense of sincerity seemed to shine from her now. She hurried around the castle, freeing all her E-Number Crew. They had never posed a real threat to anyone and were entitled to their freedom. E 131 and E 104 were the last for her to free.

"Finally free!" E 104 cried with jubilation.

"Do you need anything more from us Mam?" E 131 checked.

Miss Additive smiled. It would have been fun to say yes and order them to arrange a big party for her when this was all over, get her a new wardrobe, build her a pretty little castle where Mr Mould couldn't find her.

"No boys, you have served your time. Don't bring any further harm to the Thousand Islanders, keep to yourselves. You're free."

The two soldiers smacked each others hand in celebration and started bopping to the beats E 131 was now orchestrating. And they bopped all the way out of the castle, completely oblivious to the walls falling apart, screams of the dying E-Coli Gang or the shouts and cries as Arti chased Mr Mould.

Arti had almost caught up with Mr Mould. Ginger and Kai were close behind. But as he neared, the evil dictator stopped to press his fungi filled hands into the ground. The ground suddenly began to open and a smellycopter emerged. It was a small flying object, with propellers on its head, dripping with mould.

"Oh no, quick guys" Arti urged and mustered all the strength he had to run faster.

Mr Mould stepped into the front seat and started the engine. The propeller began to whirr and smelly dust flew around the area.

"Sorry to have to leave you after such a short visit but I am sure we'll meet again. When I rule your land!" Mr Mould waved the Silver Spoon in the air as the smellycopter started to take off. Arti, Kai and Ginger still ran after in hope, throwing rocks at him.

"By the way, the internal bomb I have set should be going off in the next ten minutes. It should cover most of Mould Island, in which case I doubt I will be seeing you again!"

The smellycopter was already quite high now. Mr Mould was chuckling to himself and flourished the Silver Spoon to them one more time. Suddenly the Silver Spoon was snatched out of his hand. A long tweezer type contraption had seized it. And then bounced back into what now looked like a bright yellow flying ship above Mr

Mould's smellycopter. With pink feathers. And green pom poms. It could only belong to one person.

"You really should take more care of your silverware! But then I guess it was never yours to begin with."

Mr Nut was hanging out of the window sniggering at Mr Mould's distraught face. He had dressed for the occasion; bright blue cape and silver trousers together with a bright blue and silver jester-type hat. Al was sat in the passenger seat next to him. He was also dressed in the same uniform clearly through no choice of his own.

Mr Mould tried to level up to the flying machine but Mr Nut had obviously kitted it out with the latest technology. The machine zipped back and forwards, up and down, so quickly that there was no way for anything to keep up with it. Mr Mould attempted it a few times but only looked farcical as he kept missing them. Realising he had nothing left and that the bomb would soon explode, he decided to give up.

"Food World will never be rid of Mr Mould. I'll be back with a bigger and better army and then Thousand Island will be slave to me!"

He pressed a button which made the propeller whirr faster. Then suddenly the angle of the smellycopter changed and began to dive rapidly towards the ground from where it had emerged before Mr Nut or Arti could reach him. Mr Mould shot them an evil smile and then dived into the gaping hole. The ground immediately closed up just as Mr Nut's flying machine came thundering down and crashed straight into the solid ground. Al and Mr Nut ran out.

"Sorry Arti, I had to tell someone" Al apologised, "but I knew Mr Nut was the wisest person to ask."

Mr Nut was adjusting his jester-type hat in the mirror of his flying machine and talking to himself. Al wondered where the wisdom he had seen in his teacher had disappeared to.

"That's ok Al, you did the right thing. And you saved Thousand Island by getting the Silver Spoon back. At least we stopped Mr Mould." It was strange seeing his teacher in this environment but then, Arti thought, it was strange all of them being here. He wanted to go home. Ginger ran up to him.

"Arti, we have five minutes before everything blows up. The others are climbing on Stinky Chink, let's go!"

Only a few seconds after Stinky Chink and the flying machine had flown above the castle, a huge explosion erupted and the castle was engulfed in flames. They had just escaped.

Arti, Ginger, Kai, Ivy, Stinky Chink, Mr Nut, Al and Miss Additive were all reunited on the shores of the Fizzy Sea. Ivy and Arti rushed over to each other and before they could speak, their arms were flung around each other in the most loving hug possible.

"I'm not going to take you out again if you disappear like that!" Arti scolded.

"Well, I don't think mum or dad will let me out again if they hear what we've been up to!" They both laughed.

"I want to go home now Arti."

"Me too."

Stinky Chink bounded over to Ivy and stood beside her quietly, no thumping of his tail.

"There is one thing Arti." Arti looked at Ivy with a slightly worried expression, what was she going to ask now?

"Well Stinky Chink did save us and now he has no owner, nobody to look after him. And seeing as Kazai has become more of your pet, I'm kind of left without one."

"But Ivy, he's huge!"

"But loving."

"What about the poison?"

"I'll take him to the dentist."

"Where will he stay?"

"School fields? He can give all the kids rides in his ears."

"But Ivy..."

"I love him Arti, he's been my friend. And besides, he can fly us home."

There was nothing Arti could say to argue with that. With a nod Ivy was jumping up and down and Stinky was throwing his tail in the air.

"Right then, everyone ready to go? I've still got this to put back!" Arti said holding up the Silver Spoon. Everyone cheered. They had rescued Ivy, were taking back the Silver Spoon and finally going home.

"Where's Mr Nut, I need to see if his flying machine is fine to fly? Mr Nut?"

Mr Nut, who had spent the whole time in the yellow capsule muttering and making adjustments came out of his cabin. He was just about to respond when he stopped in shock.

"You're alive!" he exclaimed, hurrying up to where Miss Additive was standing. She seemed to be in a similar state of amazement.

"You know each other?" Ivy asked.

Busy staring into each others eyes, Mr Nut and Miss Additive did not respond.

"They're old friends from the battle of Food World" Al replied, remembering the story Mr Nut had told him in the parts store. "I think they have a lot of catching up to do!"

A few hours later, the Thousand Islanders had landed in their old neighbourhood. Mr Nut and Miss Additive had not returned to Thousand Island, choosing instead to live on the borders of Mould Island and set up something new there. The Thousand Island heroes slept so soundly most of the journey back that it all felt like a big dream when they arrived home. As it was still dark, Stinky Chink had entered unnoticed but it was clear some explaining would have to take place with the locals in the morning. Triumphant but tired, with big goodbye hugs, they all made their way home. They knew they would meet again the next day and recount the stories and events that had consumed them this past week. They knew that they had learnt a great deal and found much in themselves and each other to be proud of.

And how did Arti and his friends get the Silver Spoon safely back to the Grater away from the evil arms of Mr Mould? Well, that's another story all together.

Acknowledgements

This book is dedicated to my own little hero, Anni. Life is a great adventure with you, thank you for being the perfect little partner.

With thanks to:

My childhood heroes. Especially my dad. For all your dedication, determination and dreams – thank you for being my inspiration, for showing me adversity is part of any journey, not the end. I know my resilience and directness comes from you. I keep the book you gave me close to my heart always, almost as good as one of your hugs. To my mum - you've always encouraged me to enjoy everything life offers, to appreciate every opportunity and to love the diversity of people around us. But you've also taught me the strongest values, to try to always do things the right way. You're always by my side, I'm so proud to be like you. To my two amazing sisters, this book has evolved as our own lives have but you still mean home to me in so many ways. Both of you have given me such a colourful life full of moments that still make me smile. Thank you for everything.

This book wouldn't be complete without my wonderful husband. Thank you for your calming influence, for a life I am truly grateful for and for loving me and the crazy ideas that came as part of the package. I'll always be grateful for that chance meeting.

I'm fortunate to have been inspired and supported by so many others. I hope you all know how special you are to me.

About The Author

L. S. Bakhai has been writing since her teens and is proud to be publishing her first children's book. She studied English Literature and French at university and works in recruitment communications. She lives in London with her husband and daughter, trusted food processor and wilting tomato plant. This book is an exploration of one of her favourite subjects.

Lightning Source UK Ltd.
Milton Keynes UK
UKOW01f2322240616

277030UK00001B/4/P